YOU ARE NOW READING

THE ADVENTURES OF THE ONE ARM WONDERMOM!

WRITTEN BY KIM STUMBO AT

Kim Stumbo
The One Arm Wondermom LLC

KIM IS AN OCCUPATIONAL THERAPIST, A WIFE, A MOTHER AND... A SUPERHERO?!

SEE HER ACTS OF COURAGE SAVE LIVES AND SUMMON COURAGE IN THE PEOPLE AROUND HER. WHAT IS YOUR SUPERPOWER?

IT WAS ILLUSTRATED BY WILLIE WOFFORD. YOU CAN SEE MORE FROM HIM AT WWW.WILLIEILLUSTRATION.WEEBLY.COM

HI! MY NAME IS KIM, MOST OF THE TIME...

I'M PART SUPERHERO!

BUT I HAVE A SECRET...

I AM THE ONE ARM **WONDERMOM!!**

BEFORE THEY KNEW IT, I SHOWED THEM ALL MY POWERS

CRAWLING

SOFTBALL

PLAYING THE CELLO

DRIVING

MY PARENTS DID AN AMAZING JOB AND COULD ONLY IMAGINE WHAT I WOULD DO IN THE FUTURE.

MY MOTHER'S JOB WAS DONE ON EARTH AND HAD TO LEAVE ME WITH MEMORIES, LESSONS AND THE FEELINGS OF CONSTANT SUPPORT.

MY FUTURE I KNEW HAD CHAGED BUT I WAS READY TO EMBRACE IT.

MARRIAGE

I CONTINUED TO GROW UP WITH MY FATHER THERE SUPPORTING ME ALL THE WAY.

COLLEGE

PRACTICE

PROFESSION

MILITARY MOVES

KIDS

I WAS CONTENT USING MY SUPERPOWERS JUST WITHIN MY FAMILY, BEING A WIFE, MOM OCCUPATIONAL THERAPIST, CARING FOR AGING FAMILY.

THOUGH MY SUPERPOWERS WERE STARTING TO GET OUT OF HAND, I NEEDED TO USE THEM OUTSIDE MY FAMILY... BUT WHO WOULD NEED THEM?

I KNEW AFTER MY FATHER LEFT THE EARTH TO JOIN MY MOTHER, I WAS READY.

MY FAMILY AND I HAD A MEETING

WE DISCUSSED WHAT NEEDED TO BE DONE IN THE WORLD

WE KNEW WE COULD HELP. WE EACH HAVE SUPERPOWERS THAT WE WERE READY TO EMBRACE.

ALEX: SONIC BOOM

HAS THE ABILITY TO MOVE FASTER THAN THE SPEED OF LIGHT

A BRAIN THAT CAN SCAN THROUGH INFORMATION IN A FLASH

AND A HELPFUL SPIRIT TO SEE WHERE HELP MIGHT BE NEEDED.

EDDIE: MAJOR BRAWN

THE STRONGEST
IN OUR GROUP

CAN MOVE ANYTHING OUT OF HIS WAY
AND THE OVERCOMER OF OBSTACLES

UTILIZING HIS SPECIAL GOGGLES TO SEE ALL THE STATS OF
AN ENVIRONMENT, HE CAN ASSEMBLE ALL KINDS OF MACHINES
AND VEHICLES THAT WE CAN USE TO COMPLETE OUR MISSIONS

SAM: DR. VEIL

MASTER OF DISGUISE

DOESN'T EVEN COVER ALL OF HIS SKILLS

HE COVERS HIS TRACKS AND TRANSFORMS INTO VARIOUS PERSONAS AS NEEDED IN SITUATIONS.

HE CAN BE THE SWEETEST OR THE MOST POWERFUL ONE IN OUR BUNCH.
WATCH OUT AND DON'T LET HIM DECEIVE YOU!!

BEN: MR. INVINCIBLE

CAPTAIN OF CALM

HE IS THE FORCE WHICH BALANCES ALL OF OUR POWERS.

HE CAN CONTAIN AND COORIDINATE ALL OF OUR POWERS WITHOUT BREAKING

OUR DAY DOESN'T BEGIN AS SUPERHEROES.
WE ARE JUST NORMAL PEOPLE.

I GET MY KIDS
OFF TO SCHOOL,

MY HUSBAND SERVES
OUR COUNTRY

AND MY BOYS LEARN
NEW THINGS FROM THEIR
TEACHERS AND ENJOY
BEING KIDS.

OUR NEIGHBORHOOD IS A QUAINT SUBURB OF A LARGER METROPOLITAN.

THERE ARE LOTS OF CULTURES, PEOPLE FROM DIFFERENT AREAS AND A RANGE OF PEOPLE WHO HAVE DIFFERENT UNIQUE SKILLS

EVEN WITH ALL THE DIFFERENCES WE SEE, NOT EVERYONE UNDERSTANDS THAT DIFFERENT DOESN'T MEAN "BAD OR WEAK"

SOMETIMES, WE HAVE TO STOP AND HELP
THOSE IN NEED AND HELP THOSE WHO DON'T UNDERSTAND

ONE DAY, ALEX CAME HOME SAD AND CONCERNED.

NOBODY PLAYS WITH ME AT RECESS. THEY SAY I TALK ABOUT WEIRD STUFF...

ISN'T THAT ONE OF YOUR SUPERPOWERS? THE ABILITY TO RETAIN INFORMATION AND SHARE IT WITH OTHERS?!!

WELL...

YEAH !!!

MY TEAM WON A GAME IN GYM CLASS BECAUSE OF SOMETHING I READ ABOUT. I KNEW EXACTLY HOW TO WIN AND I LET EVERYBODY KNOW. IT WAS AWESOME!!!

THE KIDS FROM YESTERDAY MADE SURE THEY HAD ALEX ON THEIR TEAM; NO LONGER CONCERNED WITH ALL THE KNOWLEDGE HE WOULD EXPRESS AND TALK ABOUT. THEY SAW HIS SUPERPOWERS SHINE THROUGH!

AS FOR ME, I WAS HAPPY THAT ALEX WAS ABLE TO SHOW HIS SUPERPOWER TO HIS SCHOOL MATES.

PROUD MOM MOMENT!

ALEX'S EXPERIENCE IS JUST ONE OF THE MANY WE HAVE HAD OVER THE YEARS.

~ FLASH BACK ~

GROWING UP, I EXPERIENCED MY OWN TOUGH TIMES. LUCKILY, I KNEW BETTER THAN TO BELIEVE WHAT THOSE PEOPLE SAID

BEYOND THOSE WHO CHOSE NOT TO BE KIND WERE A TON OF KIDS, ADULTS AND FAMILY WHO BELIEVED IN ME FOR WHO I WAS, NOT BECAUSE OF MY NUB.

I WAS ABLE TO "BATTLE" THE NAY-SAYERS WITH MY CONFIDENCE SUPERPOWER AND POWER TO OVERCOME! ANY TASK THAT WAS PRESENTED TO ME, I COULD ACCOMPLISH IN MY OWN WAY.

NOT ALL "BATTLES" ARE WITH PEOPLE WHO DOUBT WHAT YOU ARE CAPABLE OF. SOMETIMES THE BATTLES ARE WITH YOURSELF AND KNOWING YOU ARE WORTH IT. YOU ARE BEAUTIFUL. YOU WILL HAVE THAT ONE SPECIAL PERSON IN YOUR LIFE.

I QUESTIONED MY ABILITIES, ESPECIALLY WHEN I BECAME A MOM. I KNEW I WOULD FIGURE IT OUT BUT WITHOUT AN EXAMPLE TO SEE, IT WAS ALL ON ME.

I HAD TO BECOME THE ONE ARM WONDERMOM.

I HAD THIS MOM THING DOWN! AND WITH THAT, MY WONDERMOM POWER BECAME A REALITY!

I'M LUCKY TO BE THE MOM TO THESE THREE SPECIAL BOYS.
EACH ONE IS UNIQUE AND HAS SHOWN THEIR OWN SPECIAL POWERS AS THEY HAVE GROWN.

ALEX'S SUPERPOWERS I MENTIONED EARLIER, HE IS ABLE TO MEMORIZE TONS OF INFORMATION AND MOVES AT THE SPEED OF LIGHT!

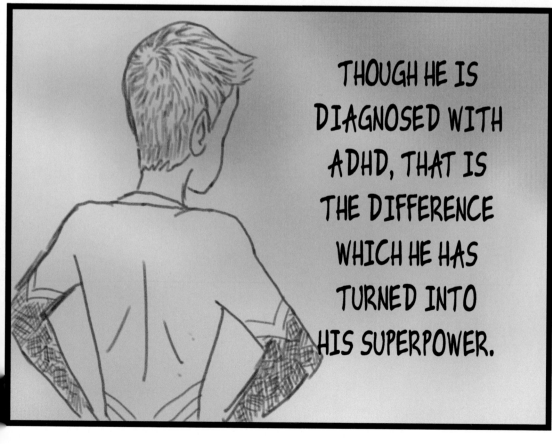

THOUGH HE IS DIAGNOSED WITH ADHD, THAT IS THE DIFFERENCE WHICH HE HAS TURNED INTO HIS SUPERPOWER.

EDDIE'S SUPERPOWER SHOWED UP AS STRENGTH AND THE ABILITY TO SEE THINGS THAT WE DON'T; LIKE THE SCHEMATICS OF OUR ENVIRONMENT OR TROUBLES THAT MAY ARISE DURING OUR ADVENTURES.

MR. INVINCIBLE AND I WERE STUNNED TO FIND OUT THAT EDDIE NEEDED GLASSES AT AGE FOUR, WHICH ISN'T A TERRIBLE THING, WHAT WE COULDN'T HAVE GUESSED WAS THAT HE WAS LEGALLY BLIND IN HIS RIGHT EYE. HIS SUPERPOWERS ALLOWED HIM TO COMPENSATE FOR THE LACK OF VISION IN HIS ONE EYE AND SEE THINGS BEYOND OUR SIGHT.

SAM CAME OUT SHOWING HIS SUPERPOWERS! SAM CAME OUT IN DISGUISE AS A FRAIL, TINY PREEMIE. THOUGH HE WAS A HAPPY, HEALTHY LITTLE BOY. SAM SPENT THE FIRST THREE MONTHS IN THIS WORLD IN NICU. HE CONTINUED TO SURPRISE AND OVERCOME HIS ROUGH START.

TODAY, SAM CONTINUES TO BE THE MASTER OF DUSGUISE SURPRISING PEOPLE EVERYWHERE WHO CAN'T BELIEVE HE WAS A 28 WEEK PREEMIE.

YOU CAN SEE HOW MY FAMILY IS HARNESSING OUR POWERS.

SUPERPOWERS COME IN SO MANY FORMS. I DON'T ALWAYS "SAVE THE DAY" FOR HUMANITY. SOMETIMES, MY SUPERPOWERS ARE NEEDED ON A SMALLER SCALE. I EXIST TO SHOW HUMANITY THAT DIFFERENT IS AWESOME, THAT ANYONE CAN DO ANYTHING THEY CHOOSE! MAYBE YOU WANT TO BE A SUPERSTAR, A MODEL, BE A ROCKSTAR OR MAYBE YOU JUST WANT TO BE JUST LIKE EVERYONE ELSE.

73042317R00018

Made in the USA
San Bernardino, CA
01 April 2018